This first edition published in the United States in 2003 by MONDO Publishing, by arrangement with Baumhaus Medien AG. Copyright © 2001 Baumhaus Medien AG, Frankfurt am Main. Written and illustrated by Klaus Baumgart.

For information contact:
MONDO Publishing
980 Avenue of the Americas
New York, NY 10018
Visit our web site at http://www.mondopub.com

Printed in the United States of America
02 03 04 05 06 07 08 09 HC 9 8 7 6 5 4 3 2 1
02 03 04 05 06 07 08 09 PB 9 8 7 6 5 4 3 2 1

ISBN 1-59034-197-X (hardcover)   ISBN 1-59034-387-5 (pbk.)

Library of Congress Cataloging-in-Publication Data

Baumgart, Klaus.
Lenny and Tweek / Klaus Baumgart
      p. cm.
   Summary: Lonely Lenny advertises for a friend, and then is surprised to find one right under his nose.
   ISBN 1-59034-197-X -- ISBN 1-59034-387-5 (pbk.)
   [1. Friendship--Fiction. 2. Animals--Fiction. 3. Birds--Fiction.] I. Title.

PZ7.B3285 Le 2002
[E]--dc21   2002023511

Designed by Edward Miller

Lenny and Tweek

by Klaus Baumgart

It started yesterday, but today the feeling was worse. Lenny was missing something.

"I need a friend. Someone I can talk to and play with!" thought Lenny.

Lenny thought and thought and thought about it some more. Then he went inside and wrote a note.

8

After a few tries, he found just the right words.

Friend Wanted:
If you are a friend, please contact Lenny.

9

Lenny took his note over to the big tree.

"I must make sure I don't hang the note too high, because my friend could be very small," he thought. "But I must also make sure I don't hang the note too low, because my friend could be very big and might not see it."

So Lenny put the note right in between too high and too low.

Lenny went home feeling very happy. He took his favorite ball out of his toy box and waited for his new friend. He waited . . .

and waited . . .

and waited some more.
But Lenny's new friend
did not come.

"Perhaps my note has fallen off of the tree and my friend can't see it," thought Lenny.

Lenny went back to the tree to make sure the note had not fallen down.

His note was still just where he'd put it. But when Lenny turned to go home, he tripped over something in the tall grass.

"Sorry," said a little voice.

"I'm okay. Are you all right?" Lenny asked.

"Yes, thanks! My name is Tweek. What's your name?" said the little voice.

"I'm too busy to talk," said Lenny. "I have to go home to see if my friend is there yet."

"Oh. Can I go with you?" asked Tweek.

"Um, okay, but we need to hurry," said Lenny.

"What does your friend look like?" Tweek asked.

"I don't know," said Lenny.

"How do you know if someone is a friend?" asked Tweek.

"Um . . . a friend is someone you can play games with. Someone you can build a sand castle with. Someone you just sit and talk to or even argue with, but you still stay friends. A friend is someone you miss when he's not there," Lenny answered.

"Do you want to play while we wait?" asked Tweek.

"Okay!" answered Lenny.

Lenny and Tweek played
hide-and-seek . . .

searched for buried treasure...

took a ride in Lenny's airplane . . .

dove into the pond . . .

stared up at the clouds...

and made chocolate-carrot pudding.

"Chocolate pudding is good if you add carrots to it," said Lenny.

"Really?" asked Tweek. "I like my chocolate pudding with peas."

Lenny and Tweek watched the sun set through Lenny's old TV. When it started to get dark, Tweek said, "It's time for me to go home. I'm sorry that your friend didn't come to see you."

"Me, too," said Lenny.

But then, a good friend would miss you too much
if he were gone for too long . . . wouldn't he?

"Do you want to play pirates, Lenny?" asked
Tweek.

As Lenny watched Tweek walk away, he realized something. "Wait a minute! Stop!" Lenny yelled as he jumped up to look for Tweek. "My friend did come to see me! You are my friend!"

Tweek was already gone.